Worried Arthur

Ladybird books are widely available, but in case of difficulty may be ordered by post or telephone from:
Ladybird Books – Cash Sales Department Littlegate Road Paignton Devon TQ3 3BE Telephone 01803 554761

A catalogue record for this book is available from the British Library

Published by Ladybird Books Ltd Loughborough Leicestershire UK
Ladybird Books Inc Auburn Maine 04210 USA

Worried Arthur

by Joan Stimson
illustrated by Jan Lewis

Ladybird

Arthur was a penguin and a worrier.

Arthur worried about whether he would grow as tall as his father...

he worried because his hair stood on end...

and now, of all things, Arthur was worried about Christmas!

One day Arthur came home from school. He looked even more worried than usual.

"And what have you been doing today?" asked Dad.

"Map of the world," mumbled Arthur. He didn't sound too happy about it.

"And where do *we* live?" asked Dad. He did hope Arthur was concentrating.

"It's called Antarctica," said Arthur. "And it's near the South Pole."

"Well done, Arthur!" beamed Dad.

That night Arthur padded across the landing. He climbed onto Dad's bed and tugged at his pyjamas. "I'm worried, Dad," he whispered. Dad stopped snoring and woke up with a start.

"What is it, Arthur?"

"It's the map of the world, Dad. We live at the SOUTH Pole and Santa Claus lives at the NORTH Pole. What if he gets tired before he arrives here? What if he runs out of toys?"

"Well, you can stop worrying about THAT,"
said Dad firmly. "Santa Claus got down here all right
when I was a lad. And he still had plenty of toys left!"

Arthur looked less worried. He trotted back to bed
and fell asleep.

On the last day of term, Arthur brought home his school report. He hovered nervously while Dad read all about him.

"Well done, Arthur. You've worked hard all term. And although your writing is rather illegible, it's nothing to worry about."

That night Arthur kept his light on late. It took him a long time to find 'illegible' in his dictionary. And, when he did, it was all very worrying.

In the middle of the night Arthur padded across the landing. He shuffled round the end of Dad's bed, and biffed him on the beak.

"I'm worried, Dad," he whispered. Dad stopped snoring and woke up with a start.

"What is it, Arthur?"

"It's my writing, Dad. What if Santa Claus can't read it? What if he doesn't bring the things on my list?"

"Well, you can stop worrying about THAT," said Dad firmly. "For your information, Santa Claus is the world's leading expert on handwriting. Good heavens, he'd soon be out of a job if he couldn't read double dutch."

Arthur looked less worried, and went back to sleep.

Two days before Christmas it began to snow heavily. Dad got out Arthur's toboggan. Some of Arthur's friends came out to play and they all made a snowman together.

Arthur was tired out when he went to bed. But he still woke up worrying.

Just after midnight Arthur padded across the landing. He opened Dad's curtains. "I'm worried, Dad," he whispered. Dad stopped snoring and woke up with a start.

"Whatever is it THIS time, Arthur?"

Arthur pulled Dad over to the window. "It's the weather, Dad. It's started to snow again. What if there's great big drifts on Christmas Eve? What if Santa can't get through?"

"Well, you can stop worrying about THAT," said Dad firmly. "You don't think Santa Claus will be put off by a bit of snow, do you? Whatever do you think he's got those hulking great reindeer for?"

Arthur looked less worried, and went back to sleep.

On Christmas Eve, Dad and Arthur decorated their tree. They put their presents underneath, and Arthur wrote his labels… very clearly.

After supper Dad sat on the end of Arthur's bed and read him a story. It was Arthur's favourite, but he still looked worried.

"Now, look here, son," said Dad. "I could use a good night's sleep. So, if there's anything worrying you, you'd better get it off your chest."

"It's my room," whispered Arthur. "What if Santa Claus comes into my room and sees all my books and toys? What if he thinks I don't deserve any more?"

"Well, you can stop worrying about THAT," said Dad firmly. "If Santa Claus only brought presents to deserving children, he would only need to work part-time. But, if it makes you feel any better, we can leave him a note."

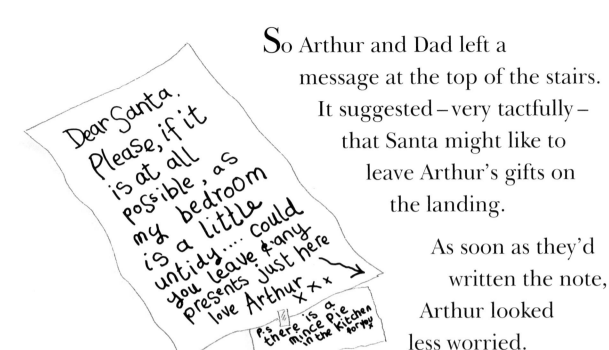

Dear Santa.
Please, if it
is at all
possible, as
my bedroom
is a little
untidy.... could
you leave & any
presents just here
love Arthur
x x x

P.s
there is a
mince pie
in the kitchen
for you

So Arthur and Dad left a
message at the top of the stairs.
It suggested – very tactfully –
that Santa might like to
leave Arthur's gifts on
the landing.

As soon as they'd
written the note,
Arthur looked
less worried.

"There's just one more thing," said Dad.

"Yes, Dad?"

"If anything else worries you in the night, Arthur,
KEEP IT TO YOURSELF until tomorrow!"

Bnut that night Arthur and Dad both slept like logs.

Next morning Arthur sat up in bed. "OUCH!"
He banged his head on the shelf above his bed.
"Yippee!" cried Arthur. "I must be growing."

He jumped out of bed and looked in the mirror.
Arthur smoothed down his hair and…
IT STAYED THERE!

Then he looked out on the landing. Sure enough, there was a stocking, filled with everything Arthur had asked for.

Arthur waited patiently for Dad to wake up. At last he came onto the landing.

"Merry Christmas, Arthur. And how are you feeling this morning?"

"I feel funny, Dad," said Arthur. Then he smiled. "It must be because…

I'M NOT WORRYING!!"